this
·little·barron's·
book belongs to

....

....

First edition for the United States and Canada published 1999 by
Barron's Educational Series, Inc.

Copyright © Penny Dann 1998

First published in Great Britain by Orchard Books in 1998.

All inquiries should be addressed to:
Barron's Educational Series, Inc.
250 Wireless Boulevard, Hauppauge, New York 11788
http://www.barronseduc.com

Library of Congress Catalog Card No.: 98-74971
International Standard Book No. 0-7641-0868-9

Printed in Italy

Five Little Ducks

Penny Dann

• little • barron's •

Five little ducks went swimming one day,
over the hills and far away.

Mother Duck said,

Quack Quack

Quack Quack

But only four little ducks came back.

Four little ducks went swimming one day,
over the hills and far away.

Mother Duck said,

Quack Quack
Quack
Quack

But only three little ducks came back.

Three little ducks went swimming one day,
over the hills and far away.

Mother Duck said,

Quack
Quack

Quack
Quack

But only two little ducks came back.

Two little ducks went swimming one day,
over the hills and far away.

Mother Duck said,

Quack Quack
Quack Quack

But only one little duck came back.

One little duck went
swimming one day,
over the hills
and far away.

Mother Duck said,

Quack
Quack

Quack
Quack

And all her five little ducks came back!